Dedicated to little artists everywhere.
Use every color you love!
—N.J.J.

To Jane and Howard for encouraging my creativity.
—C.M.

Text © 2022 by Nancy Johnson James
Illustrations © 2022 Constance Moore

Book design by Melissa Nelson Greenberg

Library of Congress Cataloging-in-Publication Data available.
ISBN: 978-1-951836-44-3

Printed in China

10 9 8 7 6 5 4 3 2 1

CAMERON KIDS is an imprint of CAMERON + COMPANY

CAMERON + COMPANY
Petaluma, California
www.cameronbooks.com

BLACK

THE MANY WONDERS OF MY WORLD

by Nancy Johnson James

illustrated by Constance Moore

cameron kids

Black is a wonderful color.

Black is every color.
Black is special. It is true.

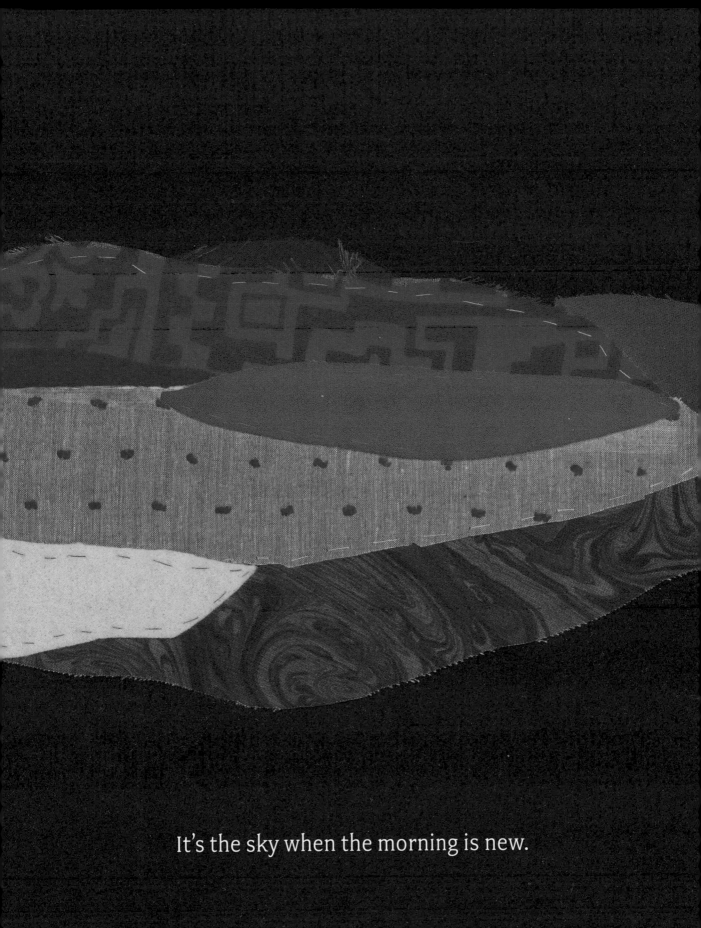

It's the sky when the morning is new.

Some people think black is scary or sad.

Some say black is heavy and bad.

I look at my world, inside and out.

I see black treasures all about.

Black is a wonderful color.

Black is the sky on starry nights.
My eyes are black—they are clear and bright.

Black is the rich, fertile earth.
And the shiny beetle tunneling dirt.

Black are intricate musical notes
and the flashing shine of fancy clothes.

Black is a wonderful color.

Black shadows dance upon the ground.
Blackbirds fly all around.

Black is a panther, strong and sleek.
Mama's braids, coiled and neat.

Black is a wonderful color.

Black is my puppy, playful and warm.

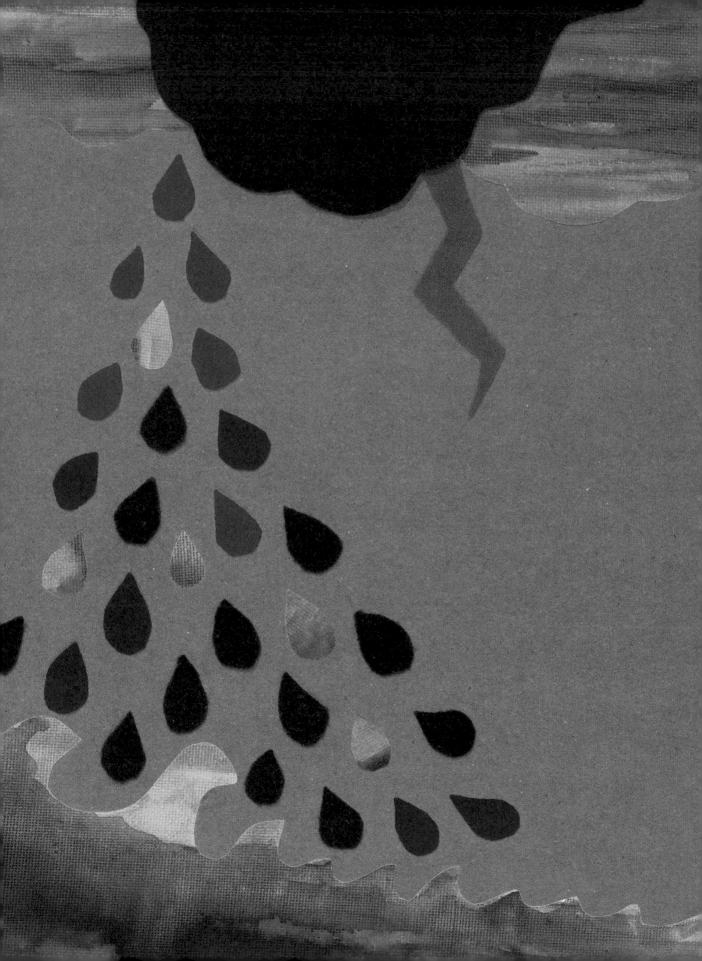

Black is the deep ocean under the storm.
Black are clouds heavy with rain
and sweet dark berries along the lane.

Black is a wonderful color.

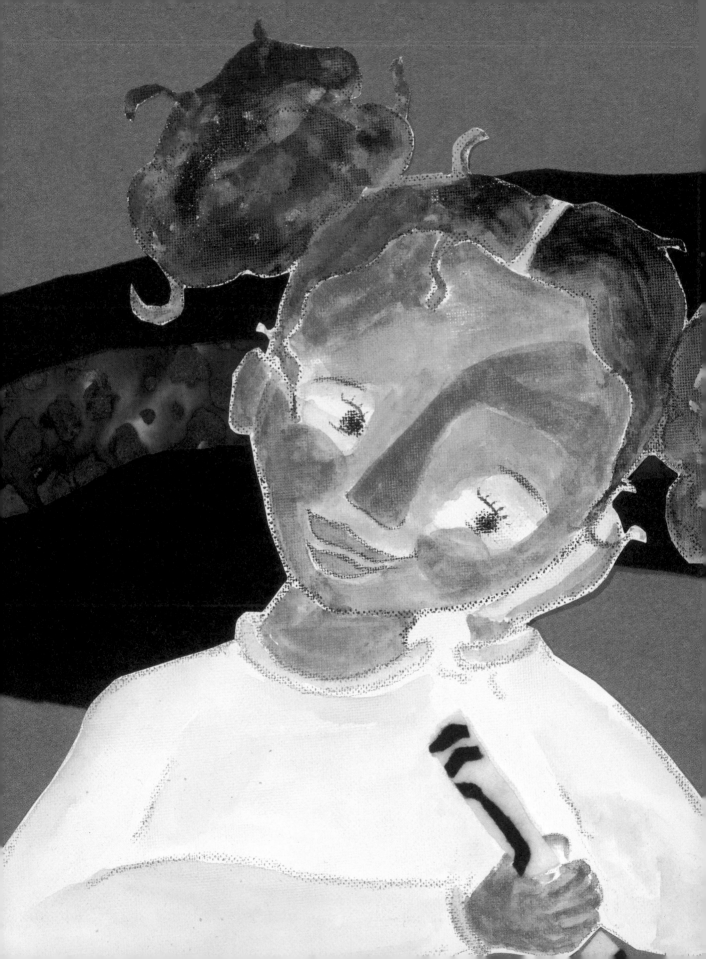

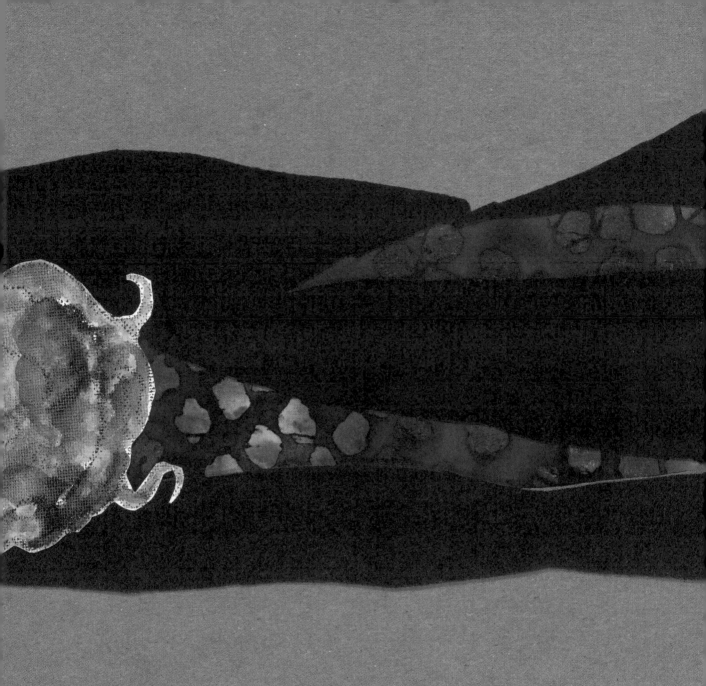

Black is the ink I use to write
and the bedroom when I turn off the light.

Black is the silence that lets me think.
Black are my eyelashes against my cheek.

Black is a wonderful color.

I dream of the beauty beyond our world.
Beyond, beyond where our planet twirls.
It's the black that was here when life began.
In the darkness of space that has no end.

Black is a wonderful color.